THE
Riddle of
Bear Cave

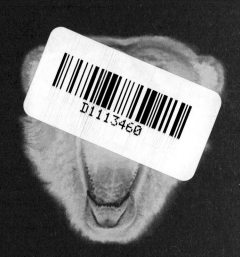

Collect all the titles in this series:

THE
Riddle of
Bear Cave

M. A. Harvey

Design & Illustration: Garry Walton

Chrysalis Children's Books

First published in the UK in 2004 by
Chrysalis Children's Books
an imprint of Chrysalis Books Group plc,
The Chrysalis Building
Bramley Road, London W10 6SP

This edition is distributed in the U.S. by Publishers Group West

Illustration by Garry Walton
Text © M.A. Harvey 2004

The right of M.A. Harvey to be identified
as the author of this work has been asserted.

ISBN 1 84458 146 2

Printed in Great Britain by Creative Print & Design (Wales) Ltd

10 9 8 7 6 5 4 3 2 1

CONTENTS

A message from

XTREME ADVENTURE IN

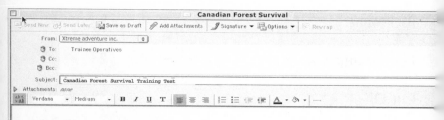

XTREME ADVENTURE INC.
confirms you are authorized to read this top secret
transmission.

To: Trainee operative.
Re: Canadian forest survival training test.

XTREME ADVENTURE INC. is an organization dedicated to
protecting the planet and those who inhabit it. Our operatives are
an elite squad who have proved their bravery, survival skills, and
brainpower. They can survive in the most dangerous, hostile
places on Earth, and we call on them for rescue missions that
are so tough that all others would fail.

Do you have what it takes to join us? We shall see.

This training manual contains an adventure story. Imagine you
became lost in an isolated forest wilderness, in danger from
grizzly bears. All that and more happened to twelve-year-old
Joe Wilson. This is his story. We will call it…

THE RIDDLE OF BEAR CAVE

WILL YOU MAKE
THE GRADE?

In each chapter of this story, there are quizzes for you to complete. They will test your brainpower and observational skills.

As you read through it, jot down of your answers to the puzzles and quizzes we have set for you.

Then check your credit score at the back of this book to see if you are capable of joining **XTREME ADVENTURE INC**.

Finally, turn to page 126 to try for a place in our ELITE SQUAD.

WARNING

Trainees who look at the answers before finishing the story will fail automatically since this shows a lack of discipline and inability to follow instructions. These are serious flaws for XTREME ADVENTURE operatives.

Good luck to all trainees.
Chief of Field Operations

Backcountry

"You're gonna love it, Joe!" Grandpa told Joe for the fourth or fifth time as they pressed their faces up against the window of their small plane. The forest below seemed to stretch on forever, a million treetops crowded side by side.

"So many trees!" gasped Joe in awe.

"That's Canada. What a country! And the best part has to be British Columbia. Can't beat it," Grandpa beamed.

Joe had never seen his Grandpa so excited and happy, and Joe himself understood because he was filled with anticipation, too. He had that almost-floating feeling you get when you know a wonderful experience is just around the corner.

All his life Joe had heard fond stories and memories set around "the family cabin." In his mind, it was a wooden dream house hidden in the depths of a magical wood. He'd never actually seen it, though. It was so far away from the city where he lived that he felt it might as well be on Mars. It was in the Backcountry, the name given to the forested wilderness of British Columbia.

"It's the best place in the world, Joe," Grandpa would say, and tell him stories about his own childhood holidays there. "Our family have owned the cabin for a long, long time. I'll take you there as soon as you're old enough and there's a big enough chunk of time for the trip."

Joe had waited impatiently for that longed-for trip to come but, up to now, there'd always been some reason why he couldn't go. His parents or his grandparents seemed too busy to schedule it. He wasn't quite sure how old he had to be anyway. He'd often ask Grandpa:

"Am I the right age yet?" and Grandpa would ruffle his hair.

"Soon, Joe," he'd say. "It's tough country up there. Beautiful but tough. You'll see."

Instead, Grandpa would take him to the park to play "survival games." They would pretend they were in the forest hunting for food or saving themselves from bears. Sometimes they'd play tracking—leaving stick arrows and secret signs around the park, using twigs and grass stalks.

Often Grandpa would tell Joe fantastic stories, such as the time he slept in a hollow under a tree root, or when he came face to face with a bear. Joe wasn't sure he really believed these tall tales, but he loved hearing them all the same.

Grandpa occasionally showed Joe a map he'd made when he was a boy. The paper it was drawn on was now yellow, with worn, fraying folds where it had been flattened and stored over the years. It indicated the best trail to the cabin, with lakes, rocks, and trees carefully marked in position.

Joe's dream of visiting had finally come true when Grandpa had announced a few weeks ago that he was ready to take his grandson to the magical world of the map. Even now, as the forest unfurled beneath their plane, it was hard to really believe that the two of them were actually on their way to the mythical cabin.

"You're sure gonna be in the sticks out here. I hope you've brought enough supplies," the plane pilot turned and remarked as they flew on and on over the real trees, rivers, lakes, and rocks scattered below. Joe thought that the landscape resembled a giant 3D version of Grandpa's old map. On the far horizon there were mountains streaked blue and black like grimy chunks of ice.

"Don't you worry about us. We'll be fine," Grandpa replied confidently.

"Sure. So you're an old-timer around these parts, huh?" the pilot added.

Joe stole a glance at Grandpa, knowing he would hate that "old-timer" crack. He wasn't that old. He was fit and very active, not like some doddering grandfather in a storybook.

Grandpa just winked at him.

"Where's your nearest store going to be?" the pilot asked.

"At Sawmill, about twenty miles south of the cabin," Grandpa explained.

The pilot nodded. "That's a long way to go for candy bars," he smiled at Joe. "Do you think you'll like it?"

"I'm gonna love it," Joe replied instantly. "I don't care about candy bars. Grandpa knows how to tap maple syrup from a tree."

The pilot laughed. Then he and Grandpa chatted away about "B.C.," as they called British Columbia.

"We had a rough winter last year," the pilot declared. "The temperature went down to almost 30 below zero. The snow was as deep as the houses, I'll tell you."

Listening to their discussion, Joe imagined what it would be like if snow fell as deep as houses in his home city. Perhaps people would build snowmen on the rooftops. He couldn't imagine a temperature as cold as minus 30.

"It must be like living inside a freezer," he

thought to himself. Joe was glad they were doing their trip in the summer.

He looked down below and couldn't see a single house for snow to cover. Then something new came into view.

"There's Sawmill," the pilot gestured out of the window toward a scar of open ground where the trees had been cleared to make a small landing strip. A settlement of wooden buildings sprawled nearby.

"Hold on. We're going down," the pilot announced. Suddenly the trees grew large and seemed to rush past the windows of the plane. Trunk after trunk whizzed by.

Bump! The plane touched down. Everything rattled, and it seemed for a minute that they were never going to stop. Joe imagined them hurtling on through the forest. But then the pilot braked and taxied to a halt.

A man in a "Forest Rescue" T-shirt and baseball cap came out of the nearest building to greet them. The T-shirt surprised Joe for a minute. He wondered who exactly the man rescued in the forest, and whether he did it a lot. It was a little worrying if you thought about it. Joe decided not to.

"Hi, Russ! Long time no see." The man greeted Grandpa with a big hug and used Grandpa's real name, which sounded odd because hardly anyone ever did in Joe's family. "So you've brought your grandson out here at last for a taste of the wilderness life," the man smiled at them.

"Yessir. Joe here is a city boy, but in three weeks I guarantee he'll be fishing and fire-building and birdwatching with the best of us," Grandpa replied and put an arm proudly around Joe's shoulder.

"How about you? We haven't seen you in a long time, Russ. Have you turned city-soft?" the man grinned mischievously.

"Never!" Grandpa insisted and they laughed together. They seemed like good friends. Grandpa introduced the man.

"This is Doug Watts. We used to play together when we were kids. He'd come out to the cabin with his dad to fish, and we'd have contests to see who caught the most."

"Your grandpa wasn't bad...for a city boy," Doug winked at Joe.

"Huh!" Grandpa huffed good humoredly, and Doug clapped him on the back.

"I took a look at your cabin a week back. It seemed fine. I stocked it up with food supplies for you. You'll need to get some more firewood during your stay, but I thought you and Joe would like to do that yourselves," Doug explained.

"Yes, that'll be fun," Grandpa grinned, and Joe agreed. He couldn't wait to start acting like a backwoodsman.

"OK, the truck's out back. Let's go," Doug declared. Grandpa squeezed Joe's arm. At last they were on their way into the magical forest!

Doug drove along a wide, rutted track deep into the trees. About an hour later, the route petered out, and Doug stopped the engine.

"We'll have to walk from here," Grandpa explained to Joe.

"OK, you take care now," Doug waved at them as they shouldered their backpacks and walked toward a narrow trail leading into the trees. "I'll be back in three weeks to bring you home. Do you have your radio?"

"I've got the cell phone, but I'm not planning on calling anyone. See you in three weeks, Doug."

Doug turned the truck and headed back in the direction of Sawmill. The dust eddied around in the light as the tires stirred it up. Then it settled; the engine noise faded and silence took over.

"Hear that?" Grandpa asked.

Joe listened.

"I can't hear a thing," he replied.

"Exactly," Grandpa smiled. "No sirens. No city traffic. Isn't it great?" The air smelled of pine needles. Grandpa took a big lungful of the air.

"Beautiful," he said, and Joe agreed. So far, the place was living up to his dream.

They walked along a narrow track until they reached the edge of a rock escarpment. From here they got an amazing view of the landscape.

The forest stretched away as far as the eye could see. In the distance, the mountains made the horizon ragged. Three different forest paths plunged down into the trees below.

Joe realized that, even though he'd never been here in his life, he knew the place as well as his own backyard. It was the place where Grandpa had sat and drawn his boyhood map. Right on cue, Grandpa took the battered piece of paper from his top pocket, smoothed it out and handed it to Joe.

"It's time to do some real-life map reading. Which way, Tracker Joe?" he grinned. "Lead me to the cabin."

ADVENTURE INC.

...e more you know about your ...ocation, the better your ...hances of survival. Try this quiz to see what you know about the northern forests of Canada. Jot down your answers and check them when you have finished the story.

XTREME ADVENTURE QUIZ 1

1. Canada is in the northern half of the world, called the Northern Hemisphere.
a) True
b) False

2. Does Canada have mountains?
a) Yes
b) No

3. British Columbia is a part of Canada. What is the wilderness in British Columbia called?
a) Backwoods country
b) Backcountry

4. What is the weather like in Canada during the winter?
a) Very cold
b) Very warm

5. Which one of these trees is found in a northern forest?
a) Spruce tree
b) Palm tree

6. West is the opposite of north on a compass.
a) True
b) False

Bear Essentials

The cabin nestled in a small clearing overhung by trees. It was simple but clean, basically one big room built from tree trunks like those that surrounded it for so many miles around. It had a porch around it and stairs that led up to a heavy door.

Joe ran his hand along the cabin's rough wall and felt the rounded shape of the logs beneath his fingers. He wondered how long they'd grown in the forest before they'd found a new home here. It might be a hundred years or more, he guessed. Inside, the cabin had a fireplace and wooden furniture, but no bathroom or kitchen. There were some boxes of food cans and bottled water, just like Doug had promised.

"This is your bunk, Joe." Grandpa showed him a neat, wooden pallet like a wide shelf. "What do you think?" Grandpa smiled and looked at Joe expectantly.

Joe breathed in the faint, mingled smells of wood smoke and resin that hung in the cabin air.

"Great!" he replied, and it was true. So far he loved everything about the place, even the fact that the curtains at the windows were faded and the windows themselves were a little dingy with dust. He'd always imagined it that way.

There was a skull mounted on the wall. It had a pair of giant antlers that were draped with wisps of dust-covered cobweb.

"That's the family moose," Grandpa grinned.

"Did you hunt it?" Joe asked.

"Nope. I think my dad bought it in a sale. When we were kids, we used to call it Mabel," Grandpa laughed. "Now, there's a few rules we need to stick to when we live in this cabin, Joe. For one thing, there's no toilet in here, not like there is in your bathroom back home. You'll have to go outside, away from the cabin, and you'll need to cover up what you've done with dirt. That means you need to take a shovel with you, OK? When you want to wash, you'll have to use some of the bottled water that Doug has left for us. But try not to waste too much. We need to conserve it for the rest of our stay."

Joe nodded. It wouldn't be as easy as life back home, but he didn't mind. It was different, that's all. He'd get used to it.

He peered out of a window, rubbing a circle through the grime with his finger and letting his imagination begin to work.

"This place would make a great hideout!" he remarked. "A gang of robbers could hide out here, no problem... Maybe a bunch of bank robbers with a stash of money!"

"There wouldn't be much to spend it on in these parts," Grandpa replied. "And those robbers would have to get out of here before the winter. That's a tough time in the Backcountry. I don't think many escaped

robbers would make it through, even inside this cabin. The snow would be so deep they wouldn't be able to get out of the door, and if they did, they'd soon freeze. If they were really unlucky they might get caught in an icicle storm. That's when long ice daggers come flying straight down from the sky!"

"Ouch," Joe winced. "Have you ever been here in the winter, Grandpa?"

"No, and I'd never care to try it," Grandpa shook his head. "But those robbers of yours would be OK in the summer if they didn't go encouraging bears. That's what we're aiming to avoid, too."

"What kind of bear is this?" Joe asked, pointing to a moth-eaten rug on the floor of the cabin. He crouched down and touched the brownish-black fur lightly with his fingers. It felt soft and cold.

"I used to call this fellow 'old grizzly' when I was a boy, but it's not a grizzly. This is the pelt of a black bear. It's smaller and has a different kind of face," Grandpa explained. He bent down and stroked the head of the rug as if it was an old pet.

"This bear died long ago, but live bears aren't so soft and harmless. Remember that bears have one aim in life: to find food. They can smell it from around a mountain, seems like. If we left food out, they'd come along, sure enough. But if we store things properly, they won't bother us. One way to store food out in the forest is to use these."

He rolled out a couple of plastic drums from under a table. They were tied with rope. He lifted one and took it outside, motioning Joe to follow.

"The rope is for stringing the drums up on branches, like this," he declared, throwing an end of rope over a branch and hauling on it to raise one of the barrels up in the air.

"It's a good way to keep food safe if you're camping out, although you have to hang them pretty far out from the trunk, because black bears can climb," he added.

"What about grizzlies?" Joe asked.

"Ah, now they can't climb, but they can reach up a long way on their hind legs," Grandpa explained, hoisting the barrel higher.

"Wow! Are they that persistent?" Joe gasped.

"You'd better believe it," Grandpa nodded. "I'll tell you something. To be a good survivor out here in the wilderness, you need to be determined and smart, and you need to adapt your thinking to your situation. Bears are just about the best example of that. They're smart and adaptable at figuring out ways to get to a meal."

Grandpa rummaged in one of his pockets and took out something shiny.

"This is for you," he smiled and handed it to Joe.

"It's a bear whistle!" Joe exclaimed.

"That's right. It's yours to keep. Bears don't like noise, so blow on it every now and then when you're out on the trail. You don't want to surprise a bear, because it might turn on you to defend itself. Remember that mothers are the most dangerous of all bears, because they will always attack to defend their young ones."

Joe slipped the whistle into the pocket of his

T-shirt and grinned. He guessed what was coming next—his favorite of all the lessons his Grandpa used to give him in the park back home.

Sure enough, Grandpa suddenly dropped to the floor on his stomach, covering the back of his neck with his arms. Joe laughed. They'd done this in the park a hundred times. He dropped to the floor beside Grandpa, who turned and looked expectantly at him.

"Do you remember the drill?" Grandpa asked.

Joe recited words he'd learned long ago in their city playing sessions: "If I meet a bear close-up, face to face, I play dead if it's a grizzly, or I throw my backpack to distract it while I climb a tree. If it's a black bear, I scare it away by shouting."

"Perfect," Grandpa replied. "If the bear is far enough away, back off quietly, but whatever you do, don't run. Bears can sprint really fast..."

"And never look a bear in the eye!" they both chanted together.

Grandpa chuckled. "You'll be fine, Joe. Just

don't forget your whistle," he smiled. "Now let's see what else you remember about survival. What's the best way to keep away animals and all those darned midges, too?"

"Build a fire!" Joe declared.

"That's right, Tracker Joe!" Grandpa nodded. "Come on. We'll do that outside. I want to boil some water for a hot drink."

They busied themselves collecting wood and soon had a campfire going. Then Grandpa showed Joe how to hang a cooking pot above the fire, on a branch suspended between two forked sticks.

It was soon evening. Sparks from the fire glowed red as they floated up against a background of shadows. Grandpa and Joe sat drinking mugs of hot chocolate.

"When we've finished out here, you'll be the best forest ranger boy there ever was," Grandpa announced. "I'll show you which berries to collect and which ones to leave on the bush, and how to make fish hooks, and coffee from acorns... Oh, and how to make a bowl from tree bark..."

Suddenly, there was a hollow whistle, followed by another and another, and a shape flashed out of the trees. It almost brushed past Joe's head as it sped through the air in a streak of gray.

Joe rocked back on his heels, lost his balance and toppled over in surprise.

"That had ear tufts. It must have been an owl," Grandpa exclaimed. "Sassy thing! I guess we disturbed it. Are you all right?"

"Sure." Jack sat up again, a little bit shaken but more embarrassed than anything.

"I bet the Native North American tribes would say it was a forest spirit come to visit us. They used to be the only folk who lived out here in the Backcountry," Grandpa remarked.

"Would they say it was a friendly spirit, do you think?" Jack asked anxiously.

"Well, it's more complicated than that as far as I can remember," Grandpa replied. "In old Native North American legends, the spirits often changed from good to bad and back again. It's not that surprising, because the tribes that lived here knew the forest very well.

They knew it had a dark side as well as a light side."

Grandpa looked out at the black shadows now gathering around them, shadows that seemed much darker than anything Joe had ever experienced before.

"The tribes worshiped the animals of the forest, particularly the bear," Grandpa explained. "Did I ever tell you there's a very rare kind of black bear that isn't black at all? It's creamy-white. Locals call it a Spirit Bear, and they always said there was a family of Spirit Bears hereabouts. When I was a boy, I longed to see one, but I never did. According to legend, a Spirit Bear is capable of very powerful magic."

Joe wished his Grandpa hadn't started on tales of forest spirits. It made him feel a little nervous.

"OK. Let's damp this fire down and turn in." Grandpa got up. "We should never leave a fire going unattended in case we start a bigger forest fire. It's a golden rule."

He glanced at Joe and saw a hint of worry in

his grandson's face. "Don't fret, Joe. Creatures around here are more scared of you than you are of them. You'll be OK." He patted Joe on the back. "Come on in. Try out your new bunk."

Joe didn't like to tell Grandpa the owl had scared him, so he said nothing and went indoors.

He was comfortable enough in his cabin bed, but for awhile he didn't sleep. Instead, he lay awake to the sound of Grandpa's steady snoring. For so long he'd dreamed about this place and imagined what it might be like. The reality was better, but also a little bit scarier than his dreams. It was better because of the woodland sounds and smells, and the excitement of the campfire and the cabin. But it was scarier because the forest was infinitely bigger and the nighttime shadows were darker than he'd thought possible.

Suddenly he jumped. His ear caught a noise, a scrape, as if something had shifted outside. Then there was a bump. His nerves tingled. Was that a bear?

He strained to hear something. Could a bear

get through the cabin door? Did Grandpa have a hunting rifle close by?

"It was probably just a raccoon or something, or maybe it was just my dumb imagination," Joe thought to himself.

He'd never admit it to Grandpa, but stepping into this new reality had had a surprising effect he hadn't expected. It had made him just a little bit nervous...

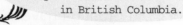

Which owl frightened Joe by the campfire? Figure out which one it was by looking at this selection of owls found in British Columbia.

Snowy Owl
No ear tufts.
White with dark spots and bar
Usually silent or shrill whis

Great Horned Owl
Dark brown and gray streaked body.
Wide ear tufts.
Calls with a long, low hoot.

Burrowing Owl
No ear tufts.
Spotted and barred.
pattern on feathers
Mellow "co-coo" call, repeated twice.

Western Screech Owl
Small ear tufts.
Overall gray with streaks and bars.
Calls with series of hollow whistles.

XTREME ADVENTURE QUIZ 2

1. Bears are omnivores. What do you think the word *omnivore* means?

a) A creature who eats plants and meat.

b) A creature who eats only meat.

2. Are bears always black?

a) Yes

b) No

3. Can bears stand on their hind legs?

a) Yes

b) No

4. Do bears have a very good sense of smell?
a) Yes
b) No

5. What kind of animal is a bear?
a) A reptile
b) A mammal

6. Can bears run fast?
a) Yes
b) No

Cut Off

The next morning, the forest seemed like a different place. Joe hadn't expected it to have so many faces. This one he loved. The air smelled fresh and full of life. Birds called between the treetops, the sun dappled the forest floor, and the trees looked stately and elegant. Some had soft, silvery bark. Others had a smooth, burnished surface.

"Most of these big trees have been here for a long, long time," Grandpa explained. "Look. I'm not giving you permission to do this. It was very bad of me, but..." He pointed around the side of a tree where some initials had been carved into the bark.

"R.W. That was you, Grandpa! Russell Wilson!" Joe exclaimed.

"Yes, I'm afraid it was. I did it when I was a boy. In those days, we didn't understand that it was wrong to damage the forest and that it needed protection," Grandpa nodded.

"But it's so quiet here. It seems miles away from harm," Joe remarked.

"Seems like it," Grandpa agreed. "As a boy I came during the Second World War. I remember thinking the troubles were a world away, as if they weren't happening, even though I knew my dad was fighting. Then I'd see a warplane flying over."

"Really?" Joe exclaimed.

"Yes, occasionally. They were U.S. planes on the way to and from bases in Alaska. I got a reminder of how things really were when I heard those engines," Grandpa replied. He put a hand on Joe's shoulder.

"My dad loved fishing. Do you want to try some today?" he asked.

"Do I!" Joe said excitedly. When he'd sat by the tiny little pond in the park back home, he'd imagined fishing in a big lake, catching fish after fish. Another part of his fantasy was about to come true.

Grandpa was obviously happy, too. He stood up, stretched, and wandered around the clearing. "I feel just like a boy again," he declared.

He didn't see the hidden tree root. Over the last few years it had crept slowly across the ground and now lay, partially hidden by earth, directly in his path. His foot snagged on it.

"Whoa!" he cried, flying over and landing heavily on his side.

"Grandpa!" Joe shouted and ran to him.

"Darn it. Ow!" Grandpa struggled to sit up.

"What hurts?" Joe asked anxiously.

"It's my ankle. I think it could be sprained." Grandpa gritted his teeth with pain.

"Could it be broken?" Joe asked.

"I don't think so," Grandpa shook his head. "Help me up, would you, Joe? Let me lean on your shoulder."

With a great deal of difficulty, Joe managed to help Grandpa up the cabin steps. Poor old

Grandpa hopped on one foot, wincing in pain, holding onto the cabin rail and then the wall, using Joe's shoulder to stop him from toppling over. Eventually, they made it inside and he lay on his bunk.

"Excuse my language, but this is a damn disaster," he barked, angry at himself for being so careless.

"Let me get your foot up...there. You're going to have to rest it," Joe muttered.

"What a fool I am," Grandpa groaned.

"Is there anything else I can do?" Joe asked worriedly. They'd never played out this scenario in the park back home.

"Can you get my cell phone? It's in my backpack. I'll phone Doug and get some help from Sawmill," Grandpa explained.

"OK," Joe agreed. He dug the cell phone out of Grandpa's backpack.

"Bring it over here. Now let me see. Shoot, it's not working," Grandpa stabbed the keypad in frustration.

"Did you leave it on?" Joe asked.

"I must've. Can you get out the spare

batteries?" Grandpa asked.

"Um, I can't find any spare batteries, Grandpa," Joe admitted. He rummaged through the contents of the backpack. "No batteries. Sorry," he said apologetically.

Grandpa sighed.

"I guess I left them at home. Your grandma will kill me," he muttered. "And your mom and dad will, too, if anything goes wrong out here." He shook his head sadly. "I should have brought an old-fashioned ham radio. Well, Joe. You're gonna have to be in charge until I can hobble around. I guess the sprain will mend in a day or two."

Joe made Grandpa comfortable with pillows. He was sure the ankle would heal quickly. It would just mean a couple of quiet days. No problem. He'd do a little exploring and help around the cabin.

"I'll tell you what, Joe. Do you think you could stoke up the campfire outside?" Grandpa asked. "If you could boil some water in that pan we used last night, I'd appreciate a cup of something."

"Sure," Joe agreed. Although he was sorry about what had happened, he felt secretly pleased by the responsibility Grandpa had given him.

He wandered around the back of the cabin, looking for logs for the fire. That was when he noticed some very disturbing signs. It looked as if maybe a bear had been nearby. How recently it had visited, he couldn't tell.

Should he warn Grandpa? He didn't want to worry him when he was laid-up. The bear had probably come awhile ago.

"I'll just keep an eye out for it," Joe thought to himself. He glanced around the clearing, took out his bear whistle and blew it.

"Joe? Are you OK?" Grandpa called.

"Just practicing," Joe reassured him.

XTREME ADVENTURE OPERATIVE FIELD TEST

If you ever camp in a forest you must make sure you don't damage the place where you are staying. Try this quiz to see if you would make a good forest tourist. Jot down your answers and check them at the end of the story.

XTREME ADVENTURE QUIZ 3

1. Should you put out your campfire before you go to bed?

a) Yes. You must never leave a fire unattended.

b) No. You should let the fire burn all the logs up.

2. What should you do with your garbage?

a) Leave it in a special bag for recycling collection.

b) Take it away with you.

3. When you leave, should you:

a) Leave the ashes of your fire in place?

b) Dig the ashes into the ground?

4. Which of these answers do you think represents the biggest danger to a Canadian forest during the summer?

a) Forest overcrowding

b) Forest fire

5. Never leave food remains at a campsite because it could:

a) Repel wildlife

b) Attract dangerous animals

6. Are all wild forest berries safe to eat?

a) Yes

b) No

Don't Run!

Grandpa didn't want his grandson to get bored while they both waited for the damaged ankle to heal. When Joe returned, Grandpa suggested some safe tasks for him to do on his own around the cabin clearing.

"Joe, you could build up the firewood store. I don't mean you should go chopping logs up, but to build a fire we'll need small pieces of wood, too. Do you think you could go and collect some branches and twigs?" Grandpa asked, then noticed that Joe looked a little troubled. "Are you all right, Joe? You look pale. Did I hear you blow your bear whistle out there a minute ago?" he asked.

"Oh...yeah, I'm fine. I was just messing around," Joe replied. He didn't want to worry Grandpa. But he was thinking to himself about the evidence of a bear visit he'd seen outside. It had really scared him for a minute, but it was pretty likely that the bear had been there awhile ago, when the cabin was deserted.

"Get a grip," he murmured to himself.

Joe felt annoyed for being so nervous and for blowing his whistle. He was determined not to succumb to paranoia about dangerous bears. Otherwise, he'd end up imagining he saw one behind every tree, and that way, he'd ruin his dream holiday.

Grandpa seemed to accept his explanation and continued talking about firewood.

"Look for dead, dry wood," he explained. "Pine, cedar, and fir branches all burn well. Oh, and you'd better change into something with long sleeves. You don't want to scratch your arms while you're rooting around."

Joe obediently changed his top. After all, Grandpa had done all this before and knew a thing or two. He was happy that Grandpa had given him the job. He was determined to shake off his silly fear of the forest, and he wanted to prove to himself he wasn't a "city-soft" coward.

Outside it was warming up. Collecting wood was going to be fairly hard work in the sunshine. He searched around the clearing and didn't find much, so he ventured through the trees a little way where it was shadier. Here he had more luck, and began to make small piles of wood that he aimed to carry back later.

It was fun to root around and then come up with a really dry-looking branch, just the right size for a fire.

"Tracker Joe. Forest Ranger," Joe murmured happily, and began a long and complicated daydream, imagining himself as a tough hero surviving in the wild, rescuing animals and tourists from raging torrents, lightning blazes, and falling trees.

Then he thought he saw the owl again, flitting above him through the trees. In his daydream, he now became a clever forest ranger tracking rare wildlife. It was fun, like the park games.

Joe tried to keep his eye on the owl and darted from tree to tree to try to catch glimpses of it. He even tried imitating the owl's soft hooting noise, as if he was an expert bird-caller.

He was deep in his fantasy when something terrifying happened that jolted him cruelly back to reality. He saw a bulky shadow move between two tree trunks about fifteen yards away.

Only it wasn't a shadow. It was solid, and it was up on its hind legs, sniffing his scent. It was hundreds of pounds of flesh, blood, claws, and fur... He had stumbled into the path of a bear.

The bear was much bigger in real life than Joe had ever imagined. It had impressively big forelegs and a slightly dish-shaped face that identified it as a grizzly bear. It was staring straight at Joe, very surprised to find him.

Joe's mouth turned super-dry. His stomach seemed to plunge down to his feet. He reached into his shirt pocket for his bear whistle, only there was no pocket and no whistle. He'd changed out of the shirt back in the cabin and left his whistle there.

"The cabin..." he thought. He glanced around. He couldn't see it, even if he felt like making a run for home, which he knew would be fatal. Running would turn on the grizzly's chase instinct, and it would easily catch up with him. Grandpa had once told him a grizzly could run fast enough to catch a horse.

"Speak softly," he murmured to himself. "OK, bear. OK, bear," he tried, but his voice came out in a high, strangled pitch.

"Don't look it in the eye," he muttered, trying hard to control himself enough to remember all the instructions he'd learned from Grandpa about meeting bears. It was easier said than done. Who could take their eyes off a potential killer in front of them? This bear could knock his head off with one swipe of its paw, if it happened to be in a bad mood. He had to hope it wasn't, or he was about to die.

He stepped back slowly and stumbled. The bear came forward. It growled and dropped on to its four feet ready for a charge.

It loped forward.
Thump. Thump.
Its weight pounded the ground.
It speeded up.
It was coming straight at him.

Which fire do you think would burn best?

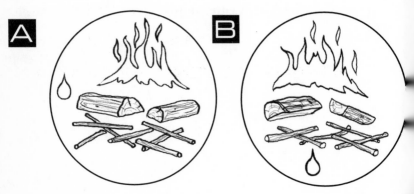

Damp logs on top of dry twigs. Dry logs on top of damp tw

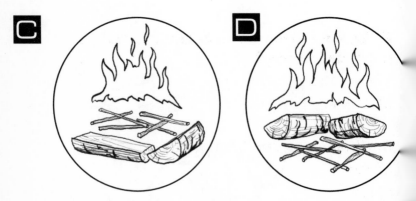

Dry logs underneath dry twigs. Dry logs on top of dry tw

What would you do if you came face to face with a bear? Try this quiz to see if you would survive. Jot down your answers and check them when you have finished the story.

XTREME ADVENTURE QUIZ 4

1. Would you stare down a bear?
a) Yes
b) No

2. Which of these two is likely to be the most dangerous?
a) A mother who has cubs nearby
b) A lone young male bear

3. Should you run from a bear?
a) Yes
b) No

4. Would you climb a tree to escape from a black bear?
a) Yes
b) No

5. How can you tell the difference between a black bear and a grizzly bear?
a) A grizzly bear has a dish-shaped face and is bigger than a black bear.
b) A black bear has a dish-shaped face and is bigger than a grizzly bear.

6. Which bear are you most likely to scare away by shouting and waving your arms?
a) A black bear
b) A grizzly bear

Losing It

Joe dropped to the floor and rolled over, face down in the dirt. He held his hands over his neck. He had to stay still and play dead. His life, his future, now depended entirely on the bear. He prayed silently.

Had he looked up, he would have seen the grizzly veer off from its fake charge. But he didn't. All he knew was that it was near. It was so close he thought he could smell its musky scent. He felt like screaming or throwing up. Was it going to bite him? Every muscle in his body tensed up.

The attack never came. Apparently the bear wasn't hungry. Perhaps it had decided that Joe was dead and not worth bothering with. Maybe it didn't like his scent. Maybe it was just Joe's lucky day...

It ambled away through the trees, and for a while Joe didn't register that it had gone. His eyes were tightly shut, and he was lying in a sweat of fear, his body filled with the reverberating, loud thump of his heart. Eventually, when he couldn't stand the silence any more, he turned his head slowly, inch by inch, until he could look up.

The bear wasn't in sight, but Joe knew it could come back. He glanced around the forest cautiously.

"Grizzlies can't climb trees," he remembered. "Or is that black bears? No, it's grizzlies," he thought, trying to focus on what he knew and stop his mind from racing in panic. He hoped with all his heart that he was right.

He picked a nearby tree with rough bark he could grasp and some likely looking footholds to help him climb. Trying to scale the tree wasn't easy, especially since he was shaking from head to foot in the aftermath of fear. His limbs felt as heavy as lead.

"Come on! Come on!" he urged himself fiercely, and that helped him make it up to a safe branch, where he was able to sit with his back against the trunk.

It was time to cry for help.

"Grandpa!" he shouted. The words died away into silence. There was no reply. When he'd been daydreaming he'd wandered a lot further from the cabin than he should have done and was too far away for Grandpa to hear him.

When he finally climbed down a couple of hours later, his limbs were stiff with tension. The grizzly bear was nowhere to be seen. It had shuffled around the area for a while, then left. That didn't mean that Joe's problems were over, though. In fact, they were multiplying. First, it was getting dark. Second, he had completely lost his sense of direction and had no idea how to get back to the cabin.

"Grandpa is going to be worried sick," he thought guiltily to himself. He imagined him trying to hobble around on his painful ankle, calling out Joe's name.

The light was disappearing quickly, and the forest had changed its face again, this time to something more sinister. Its branches looked black and spiky. Its shadows grew more impenetrable by the minute.

"Grandpa," he called out hopelessly.

He could only guess at which direction to take to get back to cabin, and he began to walk. But after an hour, it was clear he'd just made his situation a lot worse by going deeper into the forest. If only he had some equipment. He had no water, no food, and no way of knowing where he was.

He didn't want to stop searching for home but tiredness took over, and he began to stumble too often for comfort. The last thing he wanted was an injury. He realized he was going to have to rest.

Grandpa had once told Joe he'd slept the night under a tree root in the forest. Joe had never really believed him, but now it seemed like a good idea. He found a big old tree that had been partly wrenched upward in some past storm. Now its roots overhung a hollow in the ground, making a kind of roof that sheltered it from the weather.

Joe felt the ground beneath the roots. It was dry but cold, so he gathered some dry leaves and scattered them around to take away the chill. Then he climbed into the space, curled up, and tried to rest.

Sleep didn't come. He lay there with his eyes wide open, alive to every noise. Fireflies whirled past, and the trees shook their leaves in the slightest breeze. Once he thought he heard a small creature snuffling nearby. Whatever it was, it scampered away quickly as soon as it picked up his scent.

He was safe enough under the root, but inside he felt crushed.

"So much for being a hero," he thought bitterly. "Idiot, more like. Sorry, Grandpa," he muttered. His dreams of being an outstanding woodsman were shattered.

He thought about what Grandpa had said about the old Native North American legends of the forest, and how they showed that it had a bad side as well as a good side, and bad spirits as well as good.

"Congratulations, Joe. You blundered in and quickly found the bad side," Joe muttered bitterly.

It began to rain gently, splattering on the forest floor and echoing the desperate tears that were running down Joe's earth-smeared cheeks.

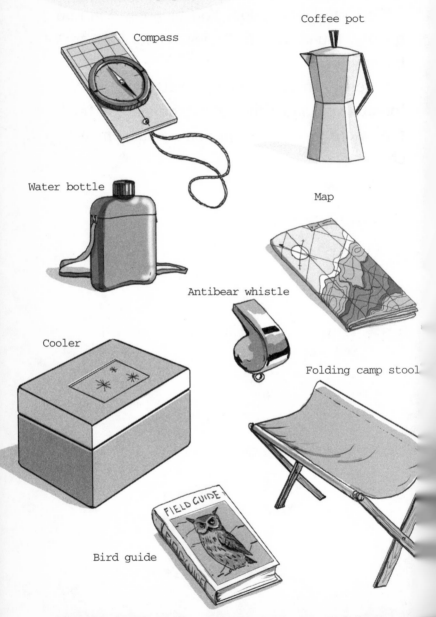

Imagine you are going on a backwoods hike. Which four vital items would you choose from this selection of equipment?

Coffee pot

Compass

Water bottle

Map

Antibear whistle

Cooler

Folding camp stool

FIELD GUIDE

Bird guide

XTREME ADVENTURE OPERATIVE FIELD TES

What would you do if you got lost in a forest? Three of the tips are correct and three are wrong. Can you pick the right ones? Check your answers at the end of the story.

XTREME ADVENTURE QUIZ 5

1. Drink any water you find.

2. Walk during the day.

3. Sit down and wait for rescue.

4. Walk through the night when it's cool.

5. Avoid drinking untreated water.

6. Leave tracking signs for others to find.

Guardian of the Cave

Dawn broke with a cacophony of bird song. The rain had stopped, and the forest pine needles were releasing their perfume. Joe's spirits were raised.

"Today I'm going to get home," he promised himself.

He heard Grandpa's voice in his mind: "You have to adapt your thinking to survive." Joe knew that's what he needed to do. He must use the information he had to plan a way forward.

"If I can't find the cabin, then the next best thing is to find the nearest community. That's Sawmill," Joe figured to himself. "I know for sure Sawmill is south of here, so if I hike south I might find someone to help me."

He nodded his head at the positive decision he'd made. It made him feel more determined.

He looked at his wristwatch.

It was 7 A.M.

The sun was up by now. He knew it rises in the east. It certainly did in the Northern Hemisphere anyway, and British Columbia was definitely a northern location. He stood up and began to look for a clearing with enough sky space for him to gauge properly the sun's position. The sun's rays helped, too. He could see their direction when they shone down through the leaves.

"If the sun is still roughly in the east, then west must be over there... And south must be that way," Joe muttered to himself. He marked what he thought was south with a stick laid on the ground.

Grandpa had taught Joe another method of finding south, and he decided to use it now to double-check his navigating. He took off his wristwatch and pointed the hour hand toward

the sun. Then he imagined a line on his watch halfway between the hour hand and the 12 o'clock mark on the watch dial. This imaginary line, he knew, would point south, and to his relief, it confirmed the position of the stick he'd laid down.

"South," he declared loudly and prepared to step forward confidently. But before he left the spot, he picked up some stones and laid them in an arrowhead shape above the stick on the ground.

"I need to leave tracking marks," he decided. He'd leave signs along the route he took, just like he and Grandpa used to do in the park back home when they were playing at being in the forest. If Grandpa had managed to raise the alarm, and someone was out looking for Joe, tracking marks might just help to lead them toward him.

His stomach grumbled. He'd had no food for awhile.

"Tough," he said firmly to himself. "You'll have to live without it." But he made a mental note to look out for some forest food, such as cloudberries, that he could safely eat to dull the hunger pangs.

A memory came into his head. His grandma had once given him a slice of pie made from cloudberries. They'd looked like small raspberries and tasted like apples, and he'd had ice cream to go with it.

"Stop thinking about food," he ordered himself out loud, and tried to put Grandma's pie out of his mind.

As he walked he "halloed" and clapped regularly to scare off any nearby bears, but much to his relief, there were no surprises today. He also regularly checked his watch by the sun to get a fix on the direction of south. Each time he did it, he left some kind of sign to show where he was going—a mark on a tree, or an arrow made of stones or pine cones. There was a chance someone might see them and, more importantly, doing it helped make him feel more positive.

"I'm going to get out of this," he told himself, and he tried to keep his spirits up by singing old songs from school and the music charts. But after awhile his energy began to flag.

All he could think about was water and food, and he was getting so obsessive about it he almost failed to notice a rockface on one side of his path. It was a little way from him and partly hidden by a tangle of shrubs, but he was sure he could make out a cave entrance underneath the foliage.

"Be careful, Joe," he whispered.

He stopped dead and watched for awhile from behind a tree. Caves were good bear dens, and this one could well be inhabited.

The worst scenario would be an aggressive mother bear with a cub to defend. If she caught his scent on the breeze, she'd come out fighting. He wouldn't stand a chance.

"Time to leave," Joe breathed.

But he hesitated. Other things in the landscape caught his eye and kept him there a moment longer, fascinated.

Near the cave entrance something stood among the shrubs. It was a thick trunk, dark and ancient, smoothed by age and no longer with branches or leaves. A contorted, angular head, with jagged teeth and bulging eyes, had been carved into the wood. Although it was lifeless, it seemed to be staring straight at Joe with unblinking ferocity.

Even more surprising, there were other signs that had evidently been placed in this landscape by people, and these were definitely not ancient signs left by Native North Americans...

Would you be good at leaving tracking signs in a forest? Try this quiz and jot down your answers. Check them when you have finished the story.

XTREME ADVENTURE QUIZ 6

1. Which would make the best tracking sign?

a) An X marked with leaves.

b) An X marked with sticks.

2. Which would make the best tracking sign?

a) An arrow made of stones.

b) An arrow made of berries.

3. Which would make the best tracking sign?

a) A knot tied in a piece of grass.

b) A pine cone stuck on the end of a stick.

4. Which would make the best tracking sign?

a) An arrow scratched on a tree trunk.

b) An arrow scratched on a stone on the ground.

5. Which would make the best tracking sign?

a) An X

b) An arrow

6. Which would make the best tracking sign?

a) A trail of flower buds placed in a line.

b) A trail of pebbles placed in a line.

Waters of Death

Mystery or no mystery, Joe realized he couldn't linger near the cave. The chances of it being a bear's den were high. He backtracked away and then tried to walk in a loop around it.

"How much farther?" he wondered. A fearful inner voice was getting louder in his mind. He was beginning to feel seriously exhausted and had a raging thirst.

"I need to rest," he thought, and right on cue, he stumbled heavily. He hit the floor painfully and sat down trying to fight back the tears.

He wiped his eyes. Through the trees, he thought he saw something reflecting light. It looked like water. He moved cautiously forward and stepped out on to the stony bank of a forest lake.

The water looked black and muddy. Dirty scum floated on the surface or washed up around its shore. There were a few patches of dead reeds and one or two rotting tree stumps on a small island in the middle. But it was water, and Joe was drawn to it.

He knew the forest rules. In his mind he could hear Grandpa explaining them:

"Don't drink water from any place you don't know is clean. If animals have dirtied it, you could be in line for beaver fever."

If Joe broke the rule and drank, he could get sick. Beaver fever was a really bad bout of stomach pains and diarrhea that would leave him helpless.

"On the other hand, without a drink I might not make it much further anyway..." Joe thought to himself.

The water lapped gently on the lake shore in the breeze. He ached for a taste of it. He knelt down and saw his face, pale and disheveled, reflected back at him. All he had to do was cup his hands and plunge them in, then lift them up to his mouth...

A momentary glance upward saved his life that day. He could never say for sure what it was that distracted him... only that it was something pale. Whatever it was, it flitted across his vision on the other side of the shore and moved his eyes from the inviting water up to the scene before him. His eyes refocused and he saw the truth.

A moose skeleton lay on the bank, as if the creature had died drinking its inviting water. Lifeless fish floated belly-up in the rotting reeds. A dead bird lay partly dragged beneath the water's surface by the weight of its waterlogged feathers.

For the first time, Joe registered the wasted branches on the overhanging trees—bleached dead wood that should have been bursting with leaves. His eyes were drawn around the lake to the right-hand bank, where they rested on a pale bulk lying along the ground. He moved toward it, and the sound of flies, growing louder as he came closer, told him that it was a dead body.

It had been a bear. Its fur, now dull and matted, had once been cream. With a gasp of shock, Joe realized that it was a dead Spirit Bear, one of the rare species Grandpa had wanted so much to see as a boy. It had once been a beautiful, strong creature, but its life had somehow been taken away by its fatal visit to the lake.

Joe crept cautiously away from the shoreline, back to where the forest grew green and healthy. There he sat pondering all the information he had.

There was a cave marked with a Native North American carving and more modern signs. There was a lake that had somehow poisoned the creatures and plants around it. Then there was Joe himself, in a very precarious position. Every decision he made now would be crucial to staying alive.

"I have to forget everything irrelevant. I have to focus on myself," he muttered.

He was feeling very weary.

"I'll rest for fifteen minutes. Then I'll keep

going," he decided. Once he'd made the choice, he stopped fighting sleep and dozed off. That's why he didn't react right away when he first heard the plane engine. It took awhile for the noise to penetrate his brain with the message that it wasn't a dream.

He opened his eyes and leapt up. A small plane was indeed overhead, but he'd lost valuable time, and its engine noise was already fading farther away.

"It could circle back. It *has* to circle back," Joe cried.

He'd played signaling games back home many times. Now he had to signal for real and think fast how to do it successfully.

Could he make a fire? He had no way of lighting it. Could he lay out a shape on the ground, using stones? There was no time for anything so complicated.

He ran back toward the lake. There he would get a clear view of the sky from the shore. On the way, he grabbed a long stick from under a tree.

Reaching the shore, he slipped off his bright-

colored shirt and tied its sleeves to the stick to make a kind of flag.

"Come back!" he shouted, straining to hear the plane engine. At last he heard it growing louder. It *was* coming back.

"Yes!" he cried joyfully. He jumped and waved his shirt wildly.

The plane buzzed overhead. Then it was gone again. There was no way of telling if it had seen him.

Now what? Should he stay put near the lake, hoping he'd been spotted? Or should he assume he hadn't been seen and keep moving, continuing to leave track marks?

If he made the wrong choice this time, he might end up dying, alone, in the forest.

He swallowed hard and sat down to wait for his fate.

XTREME ADVENTURE QUIZ 7

1. What is the name of the signaling code made up of dots and dashes?

a) Horse Code

b) Morse Code

2. It's possible to change the color of a fire smoke signal using different materials. Why would you want to do that?

a) To make it more noticeable against the background.

b) To make the fire hotter.

3. If you wanted to signal to a rescuer with a flashlight, would it be better to:

a) Keep the flashlight beam in one place.

b) Move the flashlight beam around.

4. It's a good idea to lay out a big shape on the ground for a rescuer to see. If you were to lay out a big cross-shape on the snow, would it be best to use:

a) Snowballs?

b) Sticks?

5. Do you know what the emergency signaling letters S.O.S stand for?

a) Save Our Souls

b) Security Ops Signal

6. It's important to make emergency signs that contrast the background. What does this mean?

a) Making the sign using a color that stands out well against the background.

b) Making the sign using a color that blends in well with the background.

A Shape in the Shadows

After a couple of hours, the plane had not returned and Joe was beginning to have serious doubts about his decision to stay put near the lake. If the plane had missed his shirt signal, all he had done by waiting in the same place was to lose valuable trekking time. Another hungry, thirsty night in the forest was looking increasingly likely.

"Damn. If only I could make a fire," he cursed softly to himself. Then the pilot would see the smoke if the plane went overhead again. But that plan was useless. He couldn't light a fire with no equipment, and that was that.

"What else could I use to create some sort of

signal?" he fretted.

He began to search around in the forest undergrowth, looking for some inspiration, but without food and water inside him, the effort made him dizzy. He knew that was a serious development. Once he started getting sick, he would have no chance of getting out of the forest on his own.

"Come on, Joe," he urged himself. His head swam. He almost fell over. He gulped a breath, on the verge of fainting.

It suddenly seemed as if the forest was closing around him, as if he was being shut inside a box with no escape. He sat down heavily, put a hand out, and felt the forest floor beneath him. Was he going to die here?

At that moment, he saw a shape, as white as the moon, slipping between the trees. He was certain it was a bear, yet it seemed to make no noise.

"Odd," Joe thought. The strangest thing of all was that he felt perfectly calm and unafraid. He was somehow sure that this bear was not going to attack him. It was there to help him.

His feeling of faintness melted away. Once more, the white shape flitted across his vision, and then it was gone.

There was a rustling. Twigs crackled. Then something touched his shoulder...

*

When Joe turned around, he thought he was going to look into the eyes of a bear. Instead, he saw a human, a real living, breathing man. The relief he felt was like every good thing that had ever happened to him, multiplied a thousand times.

"Joe? Are you OK? It's Doug. Doug Watts," the man spoke.

"Doug? Um...Grandpa's friend?" Joe stuttered.

"That's right. We met at the airstrip. Now sit down quietly, son. You look as if you've seen a ghost. Here, take a drink from my water bottle but not too quickly now."

Joe nodded and gratefully let the cool fresh water trickle down his throat.

"I've been out since dawn searching for you. So have the rest of the Forest Rescue Team," Doug explained. He handed Joe an energy bar from his backpack.

"Eat that. No rush. I'm going to contact the Rescue Base at Sawmill."

Doug took out a powerful radio and used it to contact the base.

"I've found him. He's OK. Tell Russ, will you?" he asked.

"Now I'm going to figure out exactly where we are," he smiled at Joe. He took out a GPS satellite navigation handset and used it to fix the coordinates of their position. When he'd done that, he put his arm around Joe.

"Feeling better?" he asked. Joe nodded.

"Your Grandpa contacted us as soon as you disappeared," Doug explained. "Well, as soon as he could get a smoking fire going. He put some old rubber tires on the flames, I think. That made a really black smoke plume that we could see for miles around. Then he sent smoke signals, just like Native North Americans used to do in the old times! When we started tracking you, we came across the signs you left. They were good. Good for you, Joe. We sent up a plane. That spotted your position, and I came to get you."

"Is Grandpa OK?" Joe asked anxiously.

"Sure is. He's hobbling a little, that's all. He'll be mighty relieved to see you, though. Can you walk? We need to hike back to the forest road to my truck," Doug said.

At that moment, Joe realized he couldn't go home. Not yet. Something had saved him. Now he had to help save the forest.

"We can't leave!" Joe declared.

Doug looked taken aback.

"What do you mean? I've got to get you checked by a doctor..." he said, puzzled.

"I know. I know. But first I have to show you something... Something important. Please, Doug," Joe insisted.

Doug frowned. Joe pulled at his sleeve.

"It's a matter of life or death," Joe cried as he moved toward the trees.

Doug shook his head in bewilderment. He thought at first Joe was delirious due to a lack of food, but he had seen the determination on the boy's face.

"Follow me!" Joe insisted.

He led Doug toward the lake and showed him the dead creatures and foliage.

"This is serious pollution," Doug muttered.

"Look at this," Joe whispered, gesturing toward the dead Spirit Bear.

Doug gasped with surprise.

"That was a truly rare creature. How sad that it's gone," he muttered angrily. "We've got to stop this death from spreading."

He radioed back to base, giving them the lake coordinates and explaining the scene.

"We've got a problem out here," he confirmed over the radio frequency. "Can someone call the forest authorities? We'll need some pollution experts to sort this one out, and we'll need them fast."

"There's more to see," Joe declared, pulling Doug's arm. He led him back into the woods toward the hidden cave. He pointed out all the other mysterious markings that had been left around the area.

"That Native North American carving looks pretty old," Doug pondered. He took a closer look. "I think it shows the figure of a bear," he explained. "A carving like this is probably here because this was once some kind of sacred place. As for the other markings, now they're a real riddle."

Joe took an eager step forward.

"I'm certain the answer is in the cave," he began, but Doug grabbed his arm.

"A cave like this could well be a bear's home. We need to tread very carefully," Doug warned.

They backed off into the trees. Then Doug took out a bear whistle and, much to Joe's surprise, he also took out a handgun.

"If there's a bear in there, noise will flush it out. But it'll be pretty mad at getting disturbed and maybe frightened, too," Doug explained. "With that combination, I can't take chances."

Doug blew his whistle and hollered loudly. Then he aimed the gun steadily at the cave mouth. Joe silently prayed that they wouldn't need to use it. He didn't want to see another bear die.

There was silence in the forest. It was as if time had stood still, waiting for something to happen...

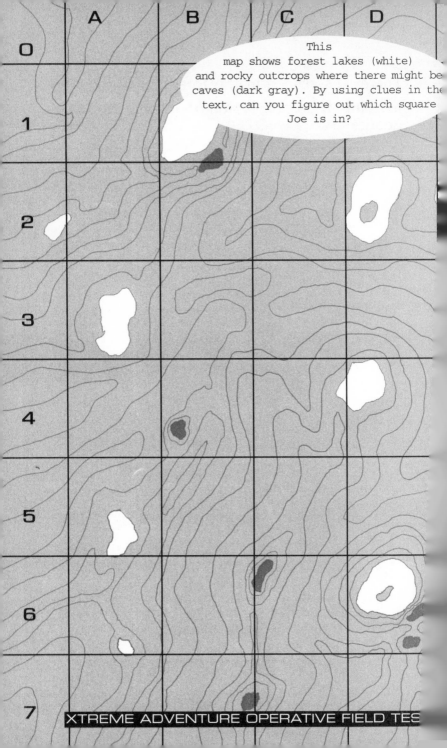

XTREME ADVENTURE QUIZ 8

1. Bears held a special place in Native North American beliefs. Were they...

a) Admired for being strong?

b) Laughed at for being weak?

2. What is a totem pole?

a) A Native North American tent pole.

b) A pole carved with mythical creatures.

3. What was a Native Indian tent called?

a) A squaw

b) A tepee

4. Native North Americans hunted elks. What is an elk?

a) A large species of deer.

b) A large species of bear.

5. What is a moccasin?

a) A type of Native North American headdress.

b) A type of Native North American shoe.

6. Native North Americans used pelts to make many things. What does the word *pelt* mean?

a) An animal skin

b) An axe

Message from the Past

No bear appeared.

"The cave is empty," Doug declared.

"Can we go in?" Joe asked. He was overwhelmed more than ever with the feeling that the cave held answers, important answers that were vital to the forest.

"OK, Tracker Joe. Follow me." Doug nodded and took out a flashlight.

The cave mouth turned out to be only an outer entrance. Inside they found another passage leading deeper into the rock. The air inside felt cool and smelled musty.

"Bears have been in here before, I'm sure of it," Doug explained, pointing to the twigs and other refuse that littered the floor of the cave.

Joe thought sadly of the pale-colored bear lying dead by the lake. Maybe this had been its home before it had taken its last fatal trip to the lakeside.

They moved again and came to an inner chamber. Doug flashed his flashlight around the walls and gasped.

"Will you look at that!" he exclaimed. Joe's mouth fell open in awe.

An image of a creature was carved on the walls, an extraordinary mythical creature with prominent claws and bulging eyes, surrounded by a swirling mass of complicated lines and patterns. Joe felt certain it was a bear.

"These must be Native North American carvings, but I've never seen anything like them before," Doug declared.

"I think it's some kind of magical place," Joe whispered. He put out his fingers, feeling an urge to touch the creature. But then he drew his fingertips away.

He didn't know how to explain his feelings to Doug, but he had the sense that this ancient art had a power that could reach him if it wished. In fact, he was sure now that it had done so in the forest, saving his life as he stooped to drink from the poisoned lake and guarding over him as he struggled alone, ready to give up. He felt that it had led him here, to this hidden chamber, and he was about to find out why.

Doug swung the flashlight down to the ground.

"Look. Over there," Joe motioned. Doug moved the light beam to focus on something that lay in the dust. Joe picked it up and held it in his palm.

"It looks like a soldier's identification tag, what they call a 'dog tag,'" Doug murmured. He looked startled, and Joe guessed why. Did that mean that someone had died in here?

Doug began to poke through the leaves and dirt on the floor.

"There are no bones as far as I can tell," he remarked. "What's this, I wonder..."

He picked up what at first looked like a leaf. But it was squared-off at the edges, the wrong

shape for a natural object. Doug squinted at it in the beam of the flashlight.

"It's a piece of paper with faded writing on it," he explained.

"Can I borrow the flashlight?" Joe asked.

"Sure," Doug agreed as he distractedly studied the scrap of paper.

Joe fell to his knees and began to search on the cave floor methodically, from side to side. As he did this, his nimble fingers found further strange evidence—four more scraps of paper and another dog tag.

"This is incredible!" Doug knelt down to see. "But I'm afraid we need to make a move now, Joe. We should try to get home before nightfall," he said, glancing at his watch.

Joe took a last look at the cave carvings. He nodded, as if to somebody or something that was there but couldn't be seen. Then he turned to follow Doug out of the cave.

"With those carvings, I'm guessing the cave was another sacred place," Doug said.

"I think they show Spirit Bears," Joe said, and Doug nodded in agreement.

"You could be right, Joe. Spirit Bears were thought of as magical. Perhaps they were once worshiped here."

He laid the mysterious pieces of paper on top of his backpack.

The writing was faded and some words were missing, but when they figured out in which order the pages went, they saw the answer to the riddle of the cave laid out before them.

The writing was a brief, scribbled account of something that had happened in this spot many years before, an event that had eventually led to death for the creatures near the lake.

"What a disaster," Doug muttered.

"A plane crashed here during the war. It was carrying deadly chemical canisters," Joe muttered as the truth sunk in.

Doug nodded. "The crew tried to leave warning signs, but my guess is that for some reason, nobody came to recover the canisters that sank in the plane wreck. The metal canisters gradually corroded over time, and now the chemicals are leaking into the water.

The lake is dying, along with everything around it," he explained.

He turned to Joe.

"You've found this forgotten lake just as the danger has begun to get really deadly. I know it sounds crazy but, well, it seems like it was almost meant to be."

He stared at Joe, who didn't reply but instead went over and touched the carving that stood outside the cave entrance. He now knew for sure that the carving showed a bear, a Spirit Bear, and he was certain that, yes, his adventure was meant to be. He'd been called by unseen forces to save this place and the forest around it. He only hoped he wasn't too late...

*

When Joe got back to Sawmill, Grandpa was waiting for him.

"Joe! I thought I'd lost you. I really did," Grandpa muttered and didn't bother to hide his tears of relief.

"I saw Spirit Bears, Grandpa. I saw a real dead one and a magic one. It floated in through the trees like an angel or a ghost," Joe explained quickly. Joe knew this sounded silly, but he also knew it was true.

"I believe you, Joe. I guess the forest gave you a special gift," Grandpa replied, hugging Joe as if he was never going to let go.

Meanwhile, Doug Watts had got on the phone to call up some urgent assistance.

"It's a big deal," Joe heard him saying.
"We'll need experts with specialist equipment, and we'll need them fast. I think that Joe has discovered this problem in the nick of time. We've got to get a move on it."

Later on, he sat with Joe and Grandpa as the last of the light faded from the forest sky.

"I hope we can get the canisters out of the lake before it is poisoned beyond any hope. The government have called in specialist help... an organization called Xtreme Adventure Inc. They'll be here tomorrow," Doug explained. Then he turned to Joe.

"You proved yourself a real forest tracker out

there, Joe. You truly did," he smiled.

Grandpa squeezed Joe's hand proudly.

"Look. A forest moon," he pointed up at the sky. "In the old times, the sky was believed to be a place where the spirits of the ancestors went. People said that if you looked closely at the moon, you would see some of them, watching over you."

Tonight the moon was bright and round, at its fullest. Joe could make out shadows and shapes spread across its surface. His science books would say that the patches were caused by the moon's mountains and valleys. But, for a moment, in the seconds before a cloud crossed over it, Joe was sure he saw the shape of a bear.

Can you figure out in which order these scraps of paper should go?

1

is a weird place. It's as though someone is watching us, yet there is nobody else here. We need to get back to base.

Jim S. 1944

2

This morning we crashed the plane. The wreckage has disappeared beneath the surface of the

3

cave near the lake. It will give us shelter, but we are afraid of bears. We cannot stay here, although that will mean leaving the poison. We are

4

lake. All the crew are OK, but the plane cargo, the canisters of chemicals, have sunk without a trace. We are going to spend the night in a

5

going to try to hike back to civilization and get help. The cave

XTREME ADVENTURE OPERATIVE FIELD TE

A good XTREME ADVENTURE operative must have a sharp memory. Find out how much you remember from the story you have just read. Jot down your answers and check them in the final section of the book.

XTREME ADVENTURE QUIZ 9

1. What was Joe's grandpa's first name?

2. What was the name of the settlement where they first landed?

3. What kind of bear charged at Joe in the forest, then veered away?

4. What piece of equipment did Joe use to confirm the direction south?

5. What crashed into the lake years before?

6. In which country is British Columbia?

XTREME ADVENTURE INC.

THE RIDDLE OF BEAR CAVE
MISSION REPORT

TOP SECRET

AUTHORIZED AGENTS ONLY

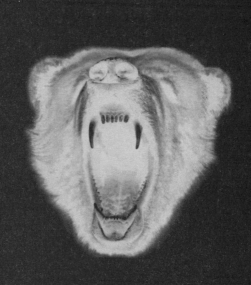

MISSION REPORT:

The forest authorities contacted XTREME
ADVENTURE INC. because we are highly
experienced at dealing with environmental
disasters quickly and efficiently. Immediate
action was necessary, so we sent in our team
of disaster specialists, along with the latest
equipment, to assess and solve the problems.

Situation judged **URGENT.**

Action taken:

The team of specialists analyzed the lake to find out exactly which dangerous chemicals they were dealing with. Then they dived underwater and raised the Second World War aircraft along with its deadly canisters. Finally, they prepared to clean up the lake.

Result:

Within a few months, the lake was safe for wildlife once more. In addition, the cave was declared a sacred Native North American site to protect it from further damage. Experts confirmed that the cave was probably an age-old place of worship sacred to the Spirit Bear, a rare form of pale-colored bear found in the forests of the Backcountry.

Research showed that, although it is rare, the Spirit Bear species still survives in this area and will receive the wildlife protection it needs.

AGENT REPORT: JOE WILSON

Joe Wilson was recommended as ideal future material for XTREME ADVENTURE INC. training. He showed practicality, bravery, and quick-thinking. He had a good memory for survival skills and adapted them to help him succeed.

Mistakes made: Joe went deep into the forest without any special survival equipment. When he got lost he was without food, water, and navigation aids.

Recommendation: During training, concentrate on equipment information.

Update: When he was old enough, Joe Wilson trained with us and became a top operative. He joined our team of ecological disaster specialists.

Location: Worldwide

Codename: Tracker Joe

Alias: Forest Ranger

AGENT REPORT: DOUG WATTS

We asked Doug to become a special
consultant, providing XTREME ADVENTURE
INC. with valuable information on wildlife and
survival techniques in the forests of British
Columbia. He has helped us to run survival
training exercises in the forest for our young
agents.

AGENT REPORT: RUSS WILSON

We asked Russ, Joe's grandfather, to help us
with forest survival training exercises for young,
would-be agents. He has proved to be an
outstanding trainer.

SPECIAL EXTRA REPORT

Our XTREME ADVENTURE agents researched
Second World War military records to find out
about the plane crash. They discovered that the
crew had indeed escaped the crash alive. They
had to survive in the wilderness for some
weeks, since at that time, there were no
settlements for hundreds of miles around.

Before they left the crash site, they put up
signs warning others of the poison in the water,
but when they finally reached civilization, they
were in a serious physical state and had lost
their maps and compasses.

As a consequence, they could never pinpoint
the site of their crash, and the plane lay
undisturbed until Joe rediscovered it.

YOUR AGENT REPORT

Did you pass the tests as well as Joe?
Score your answers to the puzzles and
quizzes. Then take the ultimate **ELITE
SQUAD** forest test on page 126.

Operative Field Test 1 (page 20)

Score 2 for the correct answer.

The answer is C, the only path with rocks to the left, trees to the right, stepping stones over a stream, and a pond to the right.

Quiz 1 Score 1 for each correct answer.
1. a) True **2.** a) Yes **3.** b) Backcountry
4. a) Very cold **5.** a) Spruce tree **6**. b) False

Operative Field Test 2 (page 36)

Score 2 for the correct answer.

A western screech owl. It called with a series of hollow whistles. It was gray and had ear tufts.

Quiz 2 Score 1 for each correct answer.
1. a) A creature who eats plants and meat
2. b) No **3.** a) Yes **4.** a) Yes **5.** b) A mammal
6. a) Yes

Operative Field Test 3 (page 46)

Score 1 for each correct answer:

There is a scratch on the wall from a creature's claws. There are bear footprints. A container has been knocked over.

Quiz 3 Score 1 for each correct answer.

1. a) Yes. You mustn't leave it unattended.
2. b) Take it away with you. There is no recycling collection in the forest!
3. b) Dig the ashes into the ground to leave the forest the way you found it.
4. b) Forest fire
5. b) It might attract dangerous animals.
6. b) No. Some forest berries are highly poisonous.

Operative Field Test 4 (page 56)

Score 2 for the correct answer:
D) Dry twigs act as kindling to get the fire going under dry logs.

Quiz 4 Score 1 for each correct answer.

1. b) No. Bears don't like being looked in the eye. **2.** a) A mother bear with cubs is very dangerous. She will attack to protect her cubs.
3. b) No. If you run, you will switch on the bear's attack instinct, and bears can run fast.
4. b) No. Black bears can climb trees. **5.** a) A grizzly bear has a dish-shaped face and is bigger than a black bear. **6.** a) A black bear.

Operative Field Test 5 (page 66)

Score 1 for each of the four correct items you chose.

The four most vital items in the list are the compass, antibear whistle, water bottle, and map. The rest are luxuries.

Quiz 5 Score 1 for each correct answer.

The correct tips are: **2)** Walk during the day when you can see dangers, such as tree roots, branches and marshes. **5)** Avoid drinking untreated water. It could make you sick. **6)** Leave tracking signs for others to find. You will increase your chances of rescue.

Operative Field Test 6 (page 76)

Score 1 for each correct answer:

a) There is a skull and crossbones carved on the post.

b) A warning and a date is carved on the rock.

c) There is a box partially hidden in the undergrowth.

Quiz 6 Score 1 for each correct answer.

1. b) An X marked with sticks. An X marked with leaves would be likely to blow away. **2.** a) An arrow made of stones. An arrow made with berries could be eaten by a forest animal such as a bird. **3.** b) A pine cone stuck on the end of a stick would be much easier to see than a knot in a piece of grass. **4.** a) An arrow scratched on a tree trunk would be easier to see, because it would be at eye level. **5.** b) An arrow would show the direction in which to go. **6.** b) A trail of pebbles would last longer than a trail of flower buds.

Operative Field Test 7 (page 86)

Score 1 for each of the four correct clues you spotted.

There are dead fish in the water, an animal skeleton on the bank, a dead bird, and dead trees around the lake.

Quiz 7 Score 1 for each correct answer.

1. b) Morse Code **2.** a) To make the fire more visible **3.** b) Move it around to make it more noticeable **4.** b) Sticks. Snowballs would not show up in the snow. **5.** a) Save Our Souls **6.** a) The sign needs to stand out clearly against the background.

Operative Field Test 8 (page 98)

Score 3 for each correct answer:

Joe is in the square 6D, the one showing a rocky outcrop near a lake with an island in the middle.

Quiz 8 Score 1 for each correct answer.

1. a) Admired for being strong

2. b) A pole carved with mythical creatures

3. b) A tepee

4. a) A large species of deer

5. b) A type of shoe

6. a) An animal skin

Operative Field Test 9 (page 110)

Score 3 for getting the order right.

The correct order is 2,4,3,5,1.

Quiz 9 Score 1 for each correct answer.

1. Russ or Russell

2. Sawmill

3. A grizzly bear

4. His wristwatch

5. A Second World War plane

6. Canada

Total up your score from a possible 80

Score of 1-30

You need to brush up on your skills. Better luck next time.

Score of 31-51

You almost made it! Try another XTREME ADVENTURE to make the grade.

Score 52-80

Congratulations. You have passed! You're good enough to be an XTREME ADVENTURE operative.

Welcome to:
XTREME ADVENTURE INC

Now you are ready to take:

THE ELITE SQUAD FOREST TEST

British Columbia is a haven for all kinds of wildlife, especially birds. Look through all the **story illustrations** in this book **(not the puzzle pages)**. Find nine birds and you qualify for our ELITE SQUAD, used for top missions.

Chris has won the holiday of lifetime
to an exotic island. On the way he
befriends the mysterious Theo.
Suddenly the holiday turns into a
nightmare when the two boys are
kidnapped at gunpoint by masked men
who abandon them on a deserted
island surrounded by sharks. Will
Chris and Theo overcome their
fears and escape from the island....
join the action and checkout
your own survival skills
in the next exciting
Xtreme Adventure Inc.

title:
The Shark Island Mystery